Poetry Three

Another Tapestry Of Words

Rona V Flynn

Thank you with all my heart
to those special friends
who have been such an
encouragement to me
and my writing

Another Tapestry Of Words

Rona V Flynn

Index

Keats or Browning

I'm no Keats or Browning,
Plath or Tennyson.
I'm not a Wordsworth or Coleridge,
Siddall or Dickinson.
I'm not a Doctor or a Scholar,
or a literary star.
I'm just me ~ will always be,
for we are who we are.

Rona V Flynn

...and that's okay.

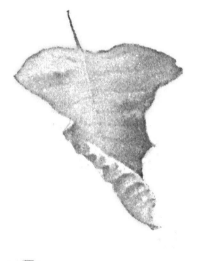

Curled Edges

Curled edges
Scuttle, scurry
Brown and crisp
Woebegone.
Tossing, turning
Veins protruding
Lines of living
Holding on.
Creeping lace
Unravelling
Fractured being
Broken one.
Fragments, traces
Crushed and shattered
Trodden, trampled
Fading
gone...

Rona V Flynn

Wild Wood

We need to get back to the wild wood,
leave the noise and the hurry behind,
breathe in the flowers and grasses,
and lose the constraints of our mind.
To discover the beauty beyond us
and nurture our heart and our soul,
we need to get back to beginning,
where nature will soothe and console.

Break free from the sounds of the city.
Come see where the sky never ends.
Let's sit by the river and listen,
begin with the healing, and mend.
We need to get back to the wild wood,
back to the place we belong.
Where chaotic beauty surrounds us,
and ministers natures sweet song.

Rona V Flynn

Low Light in September

Trees alive with fire,
deep and rich and golden
Eerie shadows, cool and long
Unhurried evening strolling
Sharp sounds and fractured light
Red sunsets, quickly gone
The promise of crisp mornings
as autumn moves along
Wispy clouds and honeyed skies
Evenings to remember
Is there anything more beautiful
than low light in September...

Rona V Flynn

Big Ted

They have such fine adventures
and he has his special place.
His arms are always open wide.
He has the kindest face.

The holder of her secrets,
he listens quietly
as they nestle in together
through life's inconsistencies.

On her sick bed he lies closely,
she holds on to his black nose.
Through their love they meld together
heart and soul, from head to toes.

He never lets her down,
and gently dries her salty tears
when the world becomes too much to bear,
assuaging all her fears.

He takes her hand quite happily,
for that's where he belongs.
They spin and dance together
as she sings her favourite songs.

The little girl, she is no more,
for time moves on so fast.
But memories of long ago
are precious, and will last.

Of eyes and ears, he now has none,
and yet he surely *sees*,
listening when her heart is sore,
with love and sympathies.

Both growing old together,
and knowing what they know.
Her constant, in a world of change ~
and ever will be so…

           Rona V Flynn

For Carol

Daydreams

We need to sit and wait sometimes,
ruminate and ponder.
Allow our thoughts to come and go,
shift and shape and wander.
A myriad of glimpses
drift across our resting mind,
random contemplations
insufficiently defined.
Time stands suspended
when we set reflections free,
from one thought to another,
riding their propensity.

Our musings will sometimes be
a stroll of slow meander,
roaming through the labyrinth
of melancholy languor.
Ambling in the distances
of half-remembered notions,
inherent perpetuity
of ever-flowing oceans.
Disembodied being,
lost in time, devoid of space.
Thinking without thinking,
as our reveries displace.

Rona V Flynn

At the age of 99,
Captain Tom Moore set out to raise one thousand pounds
for UK NHS related charities. His plan was to walk a lap of his garden every day.
He just kept going until finally hanging up his walking shoes
on his 100th birthday in April 2020.
He had raised over **32 million pounds.**
During a dark time, he captured the hearts of the nation, lifting the spirits of people around the world and spurring many on to similar ventures.
A delightful man who went on to be honoured with a Knighthood.

Captain Tom

The guards are cheering at Buckingham Palace
for Captain Tom so sweet and dear.
He has seen a hundred years
of life and love and laughs and tears.
Said the Palace.

The guards are cheering at Buckingham Palace
for Captain Tom and his garden dash.
He walked and walked to earn some cash
and shone and smiled in his silver moustache.
Said the Palace.

The guards are cheering at Buckingham Palace
for Captain Tom has a heart that glows.
Millions of pounds he's earned for those
who care for others and everyone knows.
Said the Palace.

The guards are cheering at Buckingham Palace
for Captain Tom, *Hip Hip Hooray!*
With his walk of love and his mild-mannered way,
he won our hearts and saved the day.
Said the Palace.

Rona V Flynn

Bewitched

Beneath the lamplight,
hush is falling.
Huddled together,
they peer inside ~
closely examining,
silently searching,
wide eyes imagining.
Nostrils awash
with heavenly scent,
the spell is cast.
Eyes close,
soft murmurs tumble
as raptures sweep
them into ecstasy's arms.

Rona V Flynn

It's all about a box of chocolates,
and a mother and young daughter
making their difficult choice.

He's Been on My Mind

He's been on my mind, the man on the floor
in his worn-out overcoat.
Sitting on damp hard concrete,
with a scarf wrapped round his throat.

He's been on my mind, these icy days,
when chill winds blow through the bones.
With his woolly hat and his pale blue eyes,
weathered cheeks and cold red nose.

He comes to my mind when the weather turns,
and snow clouds blow his way.
Where will he lay his head tonight
when the shops close doors for the day?

He's been on my mind, with his grey-white hair,
in waves around his face,
and his fingerless gloves holding onto the cup,
as he huddles down into his space.

He comes to my mind when I'm warm in bed
and I hear the howling storm.
Did he find a place to safely sleep?
Will he wake when daylight dawns?

Rona V Flynn

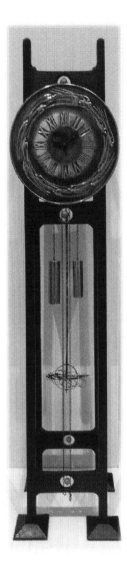

'Swallow's Flight'
Standing Clock.
Casing by
Charles Rennie Mackintosh.
Clock by Peter Wylie.

Charles
Rennie
Mackintosh

Shapes and curves.
Tall-backed chairs.
Flowing dresses.
Floating tresses.
Demure poses,
long-stemmed roses.
Glass with swirls.
Lines and furls.
Flower and leaf.
Rich motif.
Telling the story of
Mackintosh glory.

Rona V Flynn

Seasons and Signs

We know when Spring is on its way.
It's when the sun begins to stay.
It's when our bare and sleepy trees
awaken from the winter freeze.

We know when Spring is underway.
When misty cow parsley ballets
and myriads of verdant greens
fill branches with their soft new leaves.

We know when Summer's on its way.
When blossom fills the Trees of May,
and fragrant Hawthorn on the breeze
meanders through soft filigrees.

We know when Summer's here to stay,
when sun brings longer lazy days.
Sweet melodies enchant our ear
as sunlight fades and dusk draws near.

Rona V Flynn

Carcassonne ~
A medieval Citadel in south west France,
a fortress steeped in history.

Carcassonne

The citadel. A place of strength
and refuge for the Celts of Gall.
Stone steps and narrow passageways
kept them safe until their fall.
Was there ever such a damsel
with a choice of countless towers,
looking out from turrets high
across the hills and woody bowers.
Ancient chills swirl cold and sharp
between the towering grey stone walls.
Breezing through the chambers, blowing
softened whispers as they call
"Will you buy my cloth for winter?
A flagon of my finest wine
will cure all ills and keep you hail.
Best quality, these goods of mine."
Memories of a thousand tongues
lie sleeping in the cold grey stones,
spilling out when folk pass by,
rattling their long-gone bones.

Rona V Flynn

Long Love

Pure was the light that shone so bright.
reflecting well his beauty there.
With blushing lips and skin so pale,
and waves of fiery auburn hair.

I first espied him still, and sleeping
by the glassy crystal pool ~
Reclined upon the moonlit grasses
in the evening, late and cool.

He cupped his hand beneath the water
for a drink as he lay down.
Fingers playing in the moonlight
scattered silver all around.

My heart desired to reach across
the mirrored waters still and clear.
To stroke his hair while he lay sleeping,
whisper softly in his ear.

If I could cast a silver net
to turn his head and catch his eye,
that he may glance and look upon me,
then his thoughts I'd occupy.

I ached for him to turn and know
my longing for to share his breath.
I yearned to speak of endless love,
unstoppable through life and death.

I woke and watched him nimbly trace
the water's edge ~ and like a faun
his steps were light and swift and flawless,
through the mists of early dawn.

I saw him kiss the meadowsweet
and dance with joy beneath the trees.
Intoxicated, pure and free,
he frolicked with the summer breeze.

When sun was high his hair was gold,
reflected in the water's glaze,
and he would shelter with the wood nymphs
in the meadow's softened haze.

I gave the boatman all I had
and took his oars without delay.
Though waters lay as smooth as silk,
they left me wretched every day.

Bereft of strength and hope I drifted,
searching for the distant shore.
It seemed the nearer I would have him,
left me further than before.

I took my oars and rowed me swiftly
home, beneath the moonlit sky.
Once more, I watched him slumber sweetly
by the waters, and I cried.

Unattainable forever.
Destined never to be mine.
Yet still, my crushed heart lives in hope,
and will, until the end of time.

Rona V Flynn

If It's all the Same to You

We all feel hurt and happiness.
We laugh and love and weep.
Our lives unfold, our red blood flows.
We eat and dream and sleep.

When we embrace our differences,
then love alone remains.
If it's all the same to you,
I'd like to say, *We're all the same…*

Rona V Flynn

Reflections

Reflections paint a silvery film
of rippled kestrels hovering.
Sturdy boughs kneel down to kiss
the mirrors edge as shimmering
translucent skies flood the waters,
blending with the leafy hues.
Weeping willows softly sigh,
enfolded by the summer blues.

Rona V Flynn

Short Giggles

There once was a man from Pwllehli
who dated a lady called Nellie.
When the wind blew her down
to the edge of the town,
all he found was her pink spotted welly.

~

There was an old man from Black Heath
who had bother with keeping his teeth.
They weren't a good fit,
one day when he spit
they fell into the river beneath.

There was an old girl from Dundee
who spent her days watching TV.
When her batteries died,
she cried and she cried
til the vicar called in for some tea.

~

There was a wee lass from Caerphilly
who was often exceedingly silly.
She would prance and she'd dance
in fluorescent pink pants,
and her socks were incredibly frilly.

Rona V Flynn

Laughter is so good for us.

Fleeting Raptures

Soaked in sun, kaleidoscope of
rainbows scatter everywhere.
Colourful and light and bright
flimsy wings beat humid air.

Catch your breath and breathe in deep
before the colours start to fade.
Give your heart with eyes rose tinted,
blinded by the misty haze.

Wild excitement slowly yields.
Euphoria begins to tumble.
Fragile beauty falls to earth,
where wings too delicate, now crumble.

Is this where true love grows and deepens,
fluttering to solid ground?
Bathing in the everyday
of real life, with its ups and downs?

Or does love fly, escaping swiftly?
Moving on to pastures new
in search of sweet infatuation,
fleeting raptures to pursue…

Rona V Flynn

Oh, those butterflies!
What a fab feeling ~ but is it love ...

Do you ever wonder....

Face Fuzz

Sticky jam from yesterday's pud.
Crumbs from crisps in bed.
The smallest scrap of cheddar.
Brown sauce from eggy bread.

A single grain of table salt.
Froth from last night's ale,
swept along to the outer edge
like a painted dunnock's tail.

The merest trace of mustard,
darkened by its time.
And tucked away for later ~
sugar from a jellied lime.

Rona V Flynn

Be they physical or metaphorical,
we will stand before many a door in our lifetime ~
from huge and intimidating, to easy breezy.
There are doors I wish I'd opened,
and doors I wish I'd left closed.
What about you?

The Door

You stand
before the door, undecided, overdue.
Your options overwhelming
and you're not sure what to do.

You feel
preapprehension. What's on the other side?
The Bogey Man of strange and new.
Fear says run and hide.

You stop
from moving forward, a statue set in stone.
You crave all things familiar
and the warmth that comes with *known*.

You wait,
minutes take hours, whereas hours seem to fly.
White noise plagues your waking thoughts.
…To open or pass by?

You breathe.
Your mind is made up, it's just one more of more.
What's the worst thing that can happen
if you open up that door…

Rona V Flynn

The World Stood Still

The world stood still and silent.
The traders closed their doors.
Empty pavements lined dark streets
so vibrant once before.

Boxes held their people
suspended in their time,
to sit and wait and watch
the world beginning to unwind.

But unseen threads were growing
through the darkness of the day,
reaching out and touching
people safely tucked away.

And life took on new meaning
for there was more time to rest,
and to see with new perspective
things of beauty ~ and the best.

People felt much stronger
being one with many more,
and walls fell down between them
as they'd never done before.

Hearts reached out together
with their sacrificial light
and they overcame the power
of the longest, darkest night.

Rona V Flynn

Covid-19 seemed unstoppable.

But then there were...
the good, the selfless, the kindness, the ingenuity,
the sharing, the sacrifices...and the love.

So many gave their *all* for others – with some losing
their lives in the process.
They made the world a better place
during a very dark time...
and although the journey continues,
the light at the end of the tunnel
grows stronger.

I had my youngest in mind when I wrote
this poem.
If you have children in your life,
enjoy these years while you can.

Freckles and Smiles

Long skinny legs
and freckles and smiles.
Endless adventures.
Biking for miles.
Sparkling eyes.
A mischievous air.
Out all day
and never a care.
Giggles and laughter,
bright as could be.
Halcyon days
when fun was free.
Time flies swiftly.
It seems like yesterday
I left him at the school gates,
waved and walked away.

Rona V Flynn

First Grief

Twisted and wrung
from inside to out,
and put back together all wrong.
Indefinable pain.
Life isn't quite right ~
a familiar, yet discordant song.

September arrived
and his lush green life
turned to gold with the first Autumn leaves.
He quietly let go
and fell to the earth.
Leaving those who would keep him, to grieve.

Rona V Flynn

No-one is an Island

No-one is an Island,
for we do not walk alone,
we are made of the same elements of earth.
Joined inextricably,
bound from core to core,
and so, it will be true for every birth.

We will ever be connected,
and sometimes walk the steps
to reach across the chasm of reserve.
No-one is an Island,
independent and remote ~
if we look and see, then this we will observe.

One, may not have power
or the strength to stand again.
Another with another will be strong.
A fraction of the whole,
if it is lost will cause us pain,
and new life brings a new resounding song.

No-one is an Island,
we cannot exist without
the lifeblood that will run through all the parts.
To nurture well our nature,
we must recognise the whole
as not just one, but as a host of beating hearts.

Rona V Flynn

True Story...

Gypsy

She led me to the cosy hearth,
fire roaring in the darkness.
Her hair was black as coal ~
and wild, like howling winds.
Blue flowers on the tea-cup
echoed bright, her eyes so piercing.
As I sipped the strong, dark brew,
she searched my face through every word.
My final gulp was captured
by a storm of black confetti,
then she took my cup and left us.
He and me, we sat and waited.
She cast unspoken words to him,
and drew in close to show me
the dark leaves against white china.
"They say *yes,* so let it be."

Rona V Flynn

My response to an ad for accommodation led
to this unusual encounter.
The cellar was their cosy living room,
and it was there that
I drank my tea beneath the glow of gaslight ~
the tea that decided my fate that day.

FABULOUS!

Electric Sky

I don't know why
such a moody broody sky
fascinates and draws me
as storm clouds billow high.

Midnight blue and grey,
the clouds look ominous today
with rumblings and grumblings
growing louder, far away.

Swirling, hypnotizing
dark clouds keep on rising,
until thunder fills the ether
with a crash that's paralysing.

Spears of jagged white lights
shoot across the black night
with explosive blasts ensuing
to earth shattering delight.

Rona V Flynn

Tapestry

There begins to flow a river
weaving through the earthen thread,
and vibrant, living colours grow
around deep crimson red.

Past fields of lofty grasses
and trees touching the sky.
Through buttercups and daisies,
and foxgloves reaching high.

It runs dry through the desert
where rocks are scorched and bare,
then springs up in the wasteland,
bringing beauty here and there.

An oasis of abundance
fills the wilderness with song,
from the richest to the softest
as new colours flow along.

The river keeps on weaving
down the hills and through the fells,
Through valleys and dark caverns,
the woodlands, and the dells.

Growing ever richer,
the river wends its way,
with precious gold and silver
cutting through the shades of grey.

Softest silks feel gentle
to the touch, and warm and kind,
weaving through the darkness
as the colours slow unwind.

Where broken strands lie scattered
new threads mend and interweave,
creating beauty from the chaos
and a flush of verdant leaves.

A myriad of shades
gather round the darkest threads.
With yellow, green and turquoise,
weaving with the crimson reds.

Clouds of fresh wild flowers
spring beneath the lush green trees,
with lilac, pinks, and lacy whites
dancing in the breeze.

New shades of blue and violet,
with tones of golden sun,
embellish and embroider,
as the colours ramble on.

The story keeps on telling
while the threads still twist and blend
but the tapestry is richest
when the silks come to their end.

Rona V Flynn

What a journey life is!
To the silver and gold threads,
the soft, warm silks
and the beautifully embroidered colours
who have woven with me,
I say *Thank You.* x

When Benjamin Zephaniah spoke briefly about his
African origins, and the little he knows of his roots
due to slavery,
his words reached down inside me
and took hold of my soul.

Benjamin Zephaniah

They took away his culture.
They took away his name.
He will never know his roots
or breathe the smells from whence he came.

He hasn't got a history.
He hasn't got a home.
He cannot speak his joy or grief
in words that are his own.

Deep inside, his soul is yearning,
for he is bereft
of all he could and might have been ~
but there was nothing left.

They took away his language.
They made him incomplete.
He will never hold the earth
his people felt beneath their feet.

They took his true identity,
replacing it with pain.
They took away his culture.
They took away his name.

Rona V Flynn

Back of the Mind

Whatever we bind
to the back of the mind,
is sure to wake up some time.
That thing we forgot,
the which, when or what,
will elude without reason or rhyme.
It hovers just short
of cognitive thought,
never quite crossing the line.
Then, asleep in the dark,
as if touched by a spark,
it awakes as we drift into dreamtime.

Rona V Flynn

The Eyes Have It

The eyes have it,
open your mind.
Peek right inside,
see what you can find.

Encircled pools of
bottomless black
draw you in.
Will you find your way back?

Tunnels of fun
as the merry-go-rounds
blind you with lights
and hypnotic sounds.

Look through the portal,
the answer is there.
Is it laid out before you
to see? Do they care?

Be it truth or a lie,
there is something to see.
A wide open-book
or dark secrecy.

The eyes have it.
Trust in your gut.
Take time to discern
when there's something afoot.

Rona V Flynn

It's all in the eyes, Take a good look

.

Heavenly Blue

Heavenly blue,
Lift me up.
Bless me with promises,
Waft me with green and softened spring winds.

Heavenly blue,
Fill me with wonder.
Touch me and move me.
Give of your plenty and rescue me.

Heavenly blue,
Perfect and flawless.
Complete the earthen sphere.
Spread wide your canopy high above me
and make me smile...

Rona V Flynn

Intense Love

With every fibre of my being, I know it.
Like a thousand drums thundering in my ear,
Filling me with explosive light.

A floating feather wafted by certainty,
lifted by heightened emotion and power.
Tidal wave surging, by day and by night.

A storm, a tornado of spinning senses
flying me endlessly through the cosmos ~
taking me to unreachable heights.

Rona V Flynn

Hope Deferred

The joy of hope first known
brings excitement to the bones.
A lightening of the rhythm of the heart.
In time, that light grows dim
and heaviness creeps in,
seeking out that one remaining spark.

Hope gradually subsides
as expectation slowly dies.
Sun cannot warm a place that's grown too cold,
nor rain moisten the earth
to raise up the hope deferred,
where it lies still, denied the fruit as yet untold.

Rona V Flynn

In the spirit of an ancient proverb.

Virgin Beauty

Cocooned, as virgin fingers spread
a blanket, far as eye can see.
Green fields cloaked in seas of white,
wild landscapes shrouded seamlessly.

Suspended in a fantasy
of fragile crystals, natures gifts
lie swathed and veiled in mystery,
concealed by sculptured frozen drifts.

Touch has yet to mar this dream,
exquisite in the morning light,
as air hangs low across the fields
with frosted breath to kiss them white.

Rona V Flynn

Wire and Roses

Roses brush gently against hard cold steel,
wafting fragrant sweet-smelling scent.
Transient loveliness spreads and entwines
as delicate petals cover brute strength.
Slow weaving softness conceals angled edges
of fixed and immovable, silvery grey.
Rose painted picture, so tender and fragile
fades when beauty gives way to decay.

Rona V Flynn

The Skin We're In

It fits no other person
from fingertips to toes.
The shape and wrinkles
all are yours, from ears to eyes to nose.

Specifically crafted
to clothe you from outside,
whatever length or height you are ~
however slim or wide.

Your curves are carved with beauty,
be they large or small.
Hands and feet fit perfectly
however short or tall.

The sags and bags belong there,
with everything therein.
One size does not fit everyone.
Let's love the skin we're in.

Rona V Flynn

It's Cold Tonight

Iced winds blow through clear night air,
cutting to the core.
Frosted grass, like shards of glass,
stands jagged by the door.
Morning webs hang heavily
from branches by the gate.
Evening cold nips ears and nose
as breath's mist dissipates.
The moon hangs pale and distant.
Stars shine bright and clear.
Streetlamps light the jet-black night.
Winter's drawing near.

Rona V Flynn

I See Your Years are Fading

I see your years are fading,
though you still have much to say.
Impart all that you care to give,
and sit with me today.

Now take it soft and slowly ~
just stop, and talk, and be.
I'll treasure every word you give ~
as gifts from you to me.

Rona V Flynn

The longer we exist, the more we experience.
We make our way through the stuff of life,
collecting memories and maybe even enjoying
a few adventures along the way.
Without rushing and without distractions,
let's sit and listen to the heart and soul
of those who were born before us,
allowing them to impart a little of who they are.

Cascade

Swift and wild, plunging
into icy waters far below,
a thousand diamonds dance across
the surface, flying to and fro.
Sunshine flows through filtered leaves
like stars illuminating night.
Ancient rocks are shaped and honed
beneath a haze of rainbow light.

Rona V Flynn

Venus

Venus in the morning,
watches us from space.
Sailing slow across the dawn
with beauty, elegance and grace.

Twinkling after sunrise,
against the brightening sky.
Reclining near the misty moon
to share a sleepy lullaby.

Sometimes she will sparkle
with light that shines anew.
Even brighter, mega stellar!
Ineffably sublime a view.

Rona V Flynn

Caring ~ ♥ ♥ Kind~hearted ~
Thoughtful...Considerate... friendship...
..Smile Open... Kind... Freedom... warmth
On your side ~Understanding...~Love... touch...
Sweetness ~ Love ~ Care ~ Kindness ~
~Soft ~friend...Gentleness...believing Warmth. Near
...Honesty...Tenderness... Sweet...Thoughtful...
considerate Love ~ Inclusive... Love Present... Love.
InnerBeauty... Love Sensitive..Love..Honesty
compassionate... Kindness ~Generosity... Love
Listening ~ ~ Touch... Friendship...
♥Love ~ Sincerity... acceptance.
Non-judgemental... nearness..~
closeness... hearing ~♥
Trusting... heart
~Seeing
♥

Love and Friendship

Without a doubt, these words are true,
relationships need these for glue.
If we're together or apart,
these things are life-blood to the heart.

Rona V Flynn

Boudicca

She lived a life of luxury
with gold and lavish finery.
Her husband's pride and first endeavour ~
keep Iceni safe forever.

All was well, at least until
he ailed and died. For then his will
was scorned, derided, tossed aside.
His Queen deposed. Her power denied.

Filled with rage, she shared her aim
to crush the Romans, keep her reign.
Her subjects charged on battle cry
beside their Queen, to do or die.

A mighty warrior was she
who led her tribe to victory.
She overthrew the legion's best,
regained her strength to take the rest.

Though valiantly they fought the fight,
her leadership and power and might
were not enough. She was undone
and saw her people overcome.

The Iceni, alas no more,
were yielded unto Roman law.
Their kingdom seized at great a cost,
scattered, spent, a people lost.

She drank her poison, bitter-sweet,
refusing to accept defeat.
Life taken by her own fair hand ~
Her unequivocal last stand.

This tale recounts a Queen of old ~
Boudicca, the brave and bold.
She gave her all to keep her throne,
to save her people and their home.

Rona V Flynn

Boudicca was the Celtic Queen
who led the Iceni people
against the Romans, circa 60AD.
The Iceni people inhabited the northern region
of modern British East Anglia.

Softly, Softly

Slowly, slowly.
Creeping softly.
Imperceptible in time.
Roots and tendrils
soft embracing,
tight enfolding as they climb.

Gently, gently.
Ever sneaking.
Silent, lightly taking hold.
Burrowing and
all consuming,
every crack and every fold.

Softly, softly.
Wholly hiding
that which lies in dark beneath.
Covered by the
green and lovely
beauty of the ivy leaf.

Rona V Flynn

The Sweetest Hearts

The sweetest hearts breathe peace,
a little sunshine on a rainy day,
soft petals, and quiet comfort.

The softest hearts bring bluest skies,
bright eyes on a dismal day,
warmth, interest and ease.

The warmest hearts radiate
light steps of early dawn,
like sweet nectar embracing your soul.

Rona V Flynn

A Million Golden Bars

I'd give a million golden bars
to walk among the trees,
to hear the green leaves rustling
in warm mid-summer breeze.

To feel the fresh wind on my face
and touch the roughened bark.
To hear the owls twit-twooing
through the evening, into dark.

I wish these things I'd treasured
when all the days were mine.
Alas, the earth is lost to me,
for I ran out of time.

Rona V Flynn

Lazy Sunny Days

Enjoy your lazy sunny days
Ponder, breathe, relax with friends
Reminisce and laugh and love
on days you never want to end

Rona V Flynn

Meaningful time, well spent

Just a Glance

Just a glance is all it takes
for those who would imply.
Hidden from all others
with a look from eye to eye.
A private thought, a knowing,
between the two alone.
But such a glance will soon by chance
be seen, and will be known.

Rona V Flynn

Someone will always see...

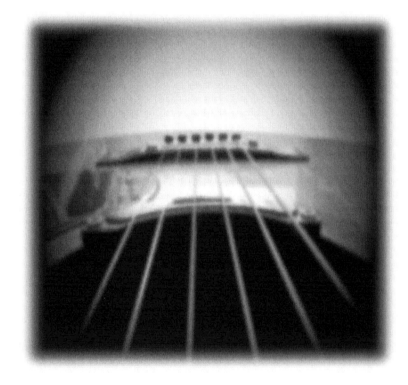

Time Travel

A random notion, like a heady potion
opens up the door.
Then we're right back there,
letting down our hair
in need of hearing more.

That warm sensation and sweet elation
when the music starts to play.
A chord, a name,
a familiar refrain
and it feels like yesterday.

Rona V Flynn

I wish you a
Blessed Christmas time
and a
Happy New Year

Christmas Limerick Silliness

Grandma opened her box
and tried on her Christmassy socks,
Grandpa said "Crikey,
they're ever so stripy
but go very well with y' frocks."

Next, it was old Uncle Fred
who put his new hat on his head.
When he saw his reflection
he voiced his objection.
It went through the window instead.

Her parcel was soft like a teddy,
but Mam said "I'm really not ready.
I know what it is,
fluffy slippers and fizz,
but me eggnog's fair knocked me unsteady."

New neighbour Ted lost his comb.
To find it, he went for a roam.
"Well now, look at that!
It's a spanking new hat!
Finders Keepers, I'm taking it 'ome."

Rona V Flynn

Enjoy some giggles this Christmas.

Brand New Year

Remember the good
and forget all the bad.
Rejoice in your friends
and the best times you've had.
Share love, peace and kindness
and lots of goodwill
and remember to always
create good times still.

Rona V Flynn

Happy New Year to you.

x

Tales

Of Wisdom

From

The Wise Counsellor

The Unexpected Gift

The sun broke free of the horizon, spreading a brightening glow as the student waited.

The Great Counsellor made himself comfortable, and began his tale…

"After filling his stomach with a good helping of his favourite food, a man sat dozing by the fire. The unexpected knock on his door irritated him, and he hesitated before heaving himself up from his easy chair to find out who was disturbing his peace. A message lay on the floor. His name was written in an unfamiliar hand, so bracing himself against the cold, he opened the door and glanced quickly up the lane, then down. There wasn't a single soul. *How intriguing,* he thought, scanning the envelope again as he quickly closed the door behind him.

Comfortably settled before his cosy fire again, he ripped the seal open and peeked inside. The bank note, nestled within the folds of a letter, made his heart leap, and an easy smile puffed up his rosy cheeks. Pausing for a few moments, he gave his best guess as to the identity of his benefactor.

Finally pulling the contents free, he gave full attention to the bank note, muttering approval when he saw the value ~ a sum not to be sniffed at. When he turned his attention to the accompanying letter, he ignored the message - darting straight to the signature. A grunt of distain escaped his lips. Tossing the crushed unread sheet into the flames, he looked again to the bank note.

Viewing it against the light of the roaring fire, he examined closely the scripted promise, illuminated by the blaze. Then, leaning slowly forwards, he touched a corner of the note to a burning coal, watching as it caught light. Turning it over and over, he sat mesmerised as the promise was slowly devoured. The colours and artistry disappeared little by little, the note blackening and twisting

103

as the flame spread. When the final glowing remnant gently floated up the hot chimney, he sniffed smugly before relaxing back into his comfortable chair. As he smiled, the rosy glow of the fire enhanced even more the sense of satisfaction he had taken from his deed."

The Great Counsellor lit the candle for a time of meditation, and they each sat quietly for a while in the growing light of morning.

The student was finally ready to speak.

'I was confused when I realised what the man intended to do. And when he took great pleasure in the burning of such a valuable gift, I thought my heart would burst. At first, he had shown much joy, but when he tossed his benefactor's message into the flames, I was truly perplexed. How would he know the words of kindness or wisdom they may have wished to share with him?

As I pondered, it saddened me that he went on to make sure the unwanted gift could not bring joy to another. Those with desperate needs in the man's own neighbourhood would have been encouraged by his generosity, and I wonder why he did not consider those without warm coats and winter boots.

Forgive me Great Counsellor, but I think it was a reckless act, and something in which he appeared to take pleasure.'

"Indeed my daughter, and have you given more consideration to these thoughts?"

'I have, but still I have found no resolution, for who would know what the man has done, except the man himself — lest he were to recount his actions to friends for amusement.'

"Child, I understand your dismay, but even *I* do not have the wisdom to know the heart of another when it is so opposed to my own. But tell me, what lesson will you take to your *own* heart from this story?"

'I have learned that the way of defiance and pride is a most unattractive path to take, and I will endeavour never to walk in it. I am also reminded to hold appreciation for all I have, and to accept and give, with grace."

"Well said, little one. We cannot truly know the soul of another, but we can learn by watching those around us. And as for you and I, time taken listening quietly to our *own* heart will help us to choose wisely."

The student smiled and nodded. *'And this I will learn to do."*

~~~

Let us not become so preoccupied with our own self-importance
that we forget who we really are.
Instead, let us consider ourselves with a sober mind,
valuing all we have,
and opening our eyes to the struggles of those around us.

The Compassionate Needs Overseer

The student dangled his feet in the water, eyes closed as he breathed in the fragrant scent of jasmine.

"Have you forgotten?" The Great Counsellor sat down beside him, smiling. "Why don't we stay here for today's lesson." And he began his tale…

"An old man fidgeted and fretted, for today he would meet the newly appointed Compassionate Needs Overseer. He would decide whether or not to allow the man's helper to stay in place, as granted by his predecessor.

The old man was frail and lived alone. When he heard the loud rap on the door, he reluctantly weaved his slight frame round the table, taking his time in an effort to delay the inevitable. His heart quickened when he glanced through a gap in the curtain. A man in a cold grey suit with a stern expression to match it, stood checking his watch.

After a brief greeting, the offer of a seat was declined. The old man hooked his cane over the back of his chair before sitting and the visitor wasted no time in beginning his questions.

Do you *this* and do you *that?* Are you *able*, are you *not?*

'I cannot get out and about.' He said. *'I find it difficult to carry shopping…I am unable to keep my home as clean and tidy as I would like, I struggle to cook a hot meal, I can walk only a short distance…'*

There were many questions but he answered each one as best he could, wondering what his visitor was thinking as he scribbled notes.

'I like it when the lady comes to help.' He wanted him to know how important his helper was. *'She brings shopping and tidies and it's pleasant to have company for a short while.'* He paused, his eyes resting on the

Overseer's expression. *He would be a good poker player,* he thought, feeling none the wiser. *'I like it when she comes, I don't see anyone, I don't have family.'*

As the old man's visitor said goodbye, he turned and smiled, leaving him surprised and hopeful as he closed the door behind him.

Later that evening the old man made his way to the inn at the end of his road. The Valley had been his local for almost sixty years, and although numbers had dwindled, he was sure to see someone he recognised on a Friday night.

At 10pm, the inn suddenly filled with younger locals who had called in to celebrate a birthday. He enjoyed watching the laughter and animated conversation – and if they noticed him, they would give him a nod and a wave, perhaps even sharing a joke with him as they passed by.

As he approached his gate, happier for having spent a little time in the warmth engaged in trivial nonsenses, he noticed the red car had gone. Shining beneath the lamplight, it had made him smile when he left earlier, for the colour reminded him of the first motorcycle he worked on as a trainee mechanic. It was old and dilapidated, but by the time he had finished it looked almost brand new. His boss said he'd never seen a trainee work so hard and he let him keep it as a reward. The memory had brought him warmth during his walk to the inn, and he had enjoyed reminiscing for a while over his drink.

~~~

After his visit to the old man, the Overseer hurried home to a delicious meal, keeping his eye on the clock as he ate – for he had an evening appointment.

He was a suspicious and determined man, and hated the idea of someone hoodwinking him. For the car the old man saw in the lamplight belonged to *him*, and he had sat for two long hours, waiting to catch him out! When he saw him finally leave his home, he punched the air in quiet triumph, watching until he disappeared into the inn. Having suspected all along he would be making his way to his local that evening, he was thrilled.

Feeling proud of himself, the Overseer returned home and poured a large glass of fine wine, complementing it with a tasty hot supper in front of the fire.

The following evening, the old man enjoyed his last hot meal. Thereafter, he would wrap himself in his overcoat before climbing into bed hungry, lonely and depressed. Sometimes he would remember the Overseer's smile as he said goodbye.

In the weeks that followed, the old man became more and more dishevelled. There was no-one to bring his shopping or clean his house, no hearty meals to heat up on cold evenings, and no cheery chatter as his helper worked - just silence and long days."

~~~

The Great Counsellor sighed, and he and his student sat quietly for a while.

The student finally spoke. '*For one man to have so much power is fearful Great Counsellor, and to use it against a weak old man is bewildering. Was it such a sin for him to seek out warmth and comfort at the inn? Why did the Overseer begrudge him precious time with the company he desperately craved? I see no evidence of compassion, a quality suggested by the Overseer's title.*

It is sad that the golden years of the old man's life would now be filled with such emptiness. Surely the Overseer created a spiral which would pull him down even further? Life had been at least bearable, with little rays of sunshine to look forward to, but now he had nothing. My heart is filled with sadness for him.'

"As is mine child, the life of one human changed by the swift stroke of a pen. Power in the hands of *One* is a dangerous thing, and something to be afraid of ~ it is a sorrow of the world around us. Although there is a lesson to be learned, we must also be heartened by the truth that more humans will choose the way of compassion."

The student smiled and nodded.

Neither felt inclined to speak further as they sat in the lengthening shadows, each with their own thoughts.

~~~

There are still good deeds in the world and
there will always be those who act with compassion.
Sometimes, we just need reminding.

Writing and Me

I first began writing after retiring earlier than expected due to voice loss. It affected everything I did, but writing was a life-saver for me.

Communication was difficult, so I decided to write a short story as a form of 'escape', and it just kept on growing. Just over three years later, I had completed *Star's Awakening* ~ my first novel. Two years on, this was followed by *The Silver Key* and the continuing story of the central family. Although I had ideas for the final novel in the trilogy, I felt the need to write something different for a while. It was then that I began to consider a poetry book.

I've written poetry off and on for most of my life, but the thought of creating a complete book of them felt daunting, and although excited, I was apprehensive. Pressing on, I set myself a target for a reasonably sized poetry book. It felt good to have a new project and I was determined to keep going until I reached that magic number.

There were frequent doubts along the way as to whether I could make it ~ But I surprised myself, and added short Tales of Wisdom to finish the book off. I couldn't believe I'd finally made it, and I enjoyed it so much I went on to write two more poetry books.

Unlike my novels, the poetry books are only available in paperback. My reasoning for this is the nature of poetry. I created the books to be held and touched ~ to keep on your shelf, and leaf through whenever the mood takes. I wanted them to be pretty too, and I consider the decorative cover, tapestry page edging, and illustrations to be part of the poetry. All of these things would be lost in an electronic copy.

Writing takes time and effort, and the creation of my books has been a huge project for me, practically, artistically and emotionally. From the blank sheet to the bound book, part of me is woven through every page.

I love it when someone says they've enjoyed one of my novels, or tells me a poem I've written is beautiful - or maybe thought provoking. I've been so encouraged by comments and appreciate the time taken when someone writes an Amazon review or gets in touch.

Time has revealed that a huge part of the process of my writing is about sharing a little of who I am. It's something we do all the time when we interact day to day with the world around us. Mixing with other people is good for us. As well as having a positive impact on our well-being, they enrich our lives and can help us to feel relevant and visible.

If you haven't tried writing, I can recommend it. Although my voice is somewhat improved (though unpredictable) I intend to continue. Writing can be fulfilling, therapeutic, challenging and satisfying ~ and if you need it to, it can give you a voice.

I hope you've enjoyed reading the poems and tales in this book, it would be lovely to hear from you.

Rona x

Please turn the page to find out more…

Snippets of Reviews

Poetry Three: Another Tapestry of Words

Long Love ~ "A beautiful poem.
Such evocative imagery…echoes of Greek myths
and all-consuming love."
Gypsy ~ " 'Like a storm of black confetti' is
one of my favourite phrases!" Cynth Browning, A Creative.

Benjamin Zephaniah ~ "Such a heartfelt and moving poem."
Susan Cole, Library Assistant

Poetry Two: Another Tapestry of Words

Damsels and Dragons ~ "A lovely poem."
The British Dragonfly Society

Blackbird ~ "A Beautiful poem. His eyes described
as 'Starlight cloaked in ebony velvet.' Gorgeous!"
Lesley Rawlinson, Author

Earth's Bones ~ "I love it!"
Jennifer Jones, Earth Scientist and Author.

Poetry: A Tapestry of Words (My first)

"Some emotive poems sparking memories; contemplation;
some smiles and some sadness."
"Beautiful and sometimes poignant."

Silver Key

"You will not be disappointed with this next book of The Light Keepers series! I absolutely loved it and was moved to tears in some parts and laughing out loud in others."

"Star's journey took us through magical portals, and introduced an array of new and interesting characters, including a couple on the dark side.

"I can't wait for the next book now, I loved reading about the struggle between darkness and light and the inner struggles of the characters. It' so true to life!"

"An enjoyable story, with a hint of a new adventure to come."

"They are absolutely brilliant books! I couldn't put them down as I was so excited to find out what happens next. I can't wait until my daughter is old enough to read them, I know she's going to love them."

Star's Awakening

"The author has created a really vivid world. The book is easy to read and nicely paced."

"I thoroughly enjoyed it. It was one of those books I just wanted to keep on turning the pages to find out what was happening next."

"I thoroughly enjoyed this book. The characters were easy to visualise."

"A good story line and great characterisation."

"I was totally drawn into the life of the central family."

"It was amazing. I absolutely loved the story line and the characters!! Can't wait for the next book in the series."

"An interesting and enjoyable read, I was drawn into the story right from the beginning."

"I was intrigued, it was complex, I couldn't put it down."

Cont'd…

Novels are available in Paperback and Kindle

Star's Awakening and The Silver Key feature the age-old struggle between good and evil, and the family's journey through it. The tales begin in Gawswood, a close-knit community with Star's family is at the heart of it.

Star's Awakening – Lightkeepers Book One
Star's widowed father is the settle Elder. All is well, but as Star prepares for her coming of age, everything begins to change. Old enemies, the discovery of family secrets, and life-changing events lead us through their journey.

The Silver Key – Lightkeepers Book Two
The continuation of *Star's Awakening* picks up the family's tale five years later. Life in Gawswood has been good - but all is not as it seems. We watch the human condition weaving its way through the trials and tribulations that beset them. Interesting new characters join them as they search for answers and closure.

Printed in Poland
by Amazon Fulfillment
Poland Sp. z o.o., Wrocław

90543225R00073